This is a work of fiction. Any references to historical events, real
people, or real places are used fictitiously. Other names, characters,
places, and events are products of the author's imagination, and any
resemblance to actual events or places or persons, living or dead, is
entirely coincidental.

 little bee books

251 Park Avenue South, New York, NY 10010
Copyright © 2020 by Little Bee Books
All rights reserved, including the right of reproduction
in whole or in part in any form.
Printed in the United States of America LSC 0620
littlebeebooks.com

Library of Congress Cataloging-in-Publication Data
is available upon request.
ISBN 978-1-4998-1106-3
First Edition 10 9 8 7 6 5 4 3 2 1

For information about special discounts on bulk purchases, please
contact Little Bee Books at sales@littlebeebooks.com.

ESCAPE FROM . . .
the Titanic

by Mary Kay Carson
illustrated by Nigel Chilvers

little bee books

1910

White Star Line Office; Liverpool, England

"Thirty-two lifeboats!" exclaims an older man standing at the head of a large wooden conference table. A gold watch chain disappears into a vest pocket of his expensive suit. In front of him are diagrams and blueprints of a large ship. Construction of the ocean liner is already underway.

"Yes, sir. We've designed the ship's deck to hold thirty-two lifeboats. That number can carry nearly two thousand people," says a younger man. His jacket is off, and his shirt sleeves are rolled up. Leather suspenders dig into his hunched shoulders.

"That many large lifeboats will cover the entire deck!" barks the suited man. "Who wants to stroll a deck weaving between ugly lifeboats? This is the world's most expensive ocean liner. White Star Line passengers are paying for luxury! They don't want to look at emergency equipment."

"It *is* a luxurious resort, sir," responds the man wearing suspenders. "There are restaurants, outdoor exercise areas, a swimming pool, and the finest dining and entertainment."

"Indeed. Well, how many lifeboats are required by law?" asks the older man.

"For a ship of this size? Sixteen or so, sir," says the younger man.

"Excellent. We will install an even twenty lifeboats," declares the older man.

"But twenty lifeboats will only accommodate one thousand, one hundred, and seventy-eight people, sir," says the younger man.

"No matter! Those lifeboats will never leave the ship. The *Titanic* is unsinkable!"

Far away, in the frigid oceans of the far north, an iceberg is being born. Its mother is a glacier: a slab of ice that inches across Greenland. Where the glacier meets the sea, chunks break off, calving icebergs. They splash and crash into the water. The icebergs bob up and float away.

One newborn iceberg is extra-huge. It floats south from Greenland with the current. The iceberg begins a two-year journey that takes it into the North Atlantic sea lanes. These are the routes ships use to travel across the ocean, including one famous ocean liner that will travel from England to America—the *Titanic*.

REALITY CHECK

WHY WERE SO FEW LIFEBOATS REQUIRED BY LAW?
England's regulations were out-of-date. An 1894 law required lifeboats for 1,060 people. By the time construction on the *Titanic* began in 1909, ships had gotten larger. The *Titanic* was big enough to carry some 3,500 people! This was many more than the law accounted for. There were over 2,200 passengers and crew on its maiden voyage.

Map of the *Titanic*

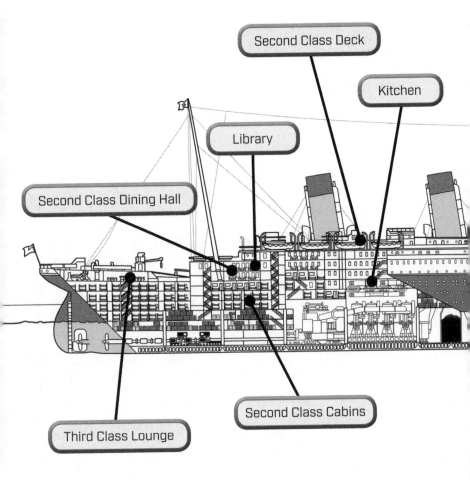

Second Class Deck

Kitchen

Library

Second Class Dining Hall

Third Class Lounge

Second Class Cabins

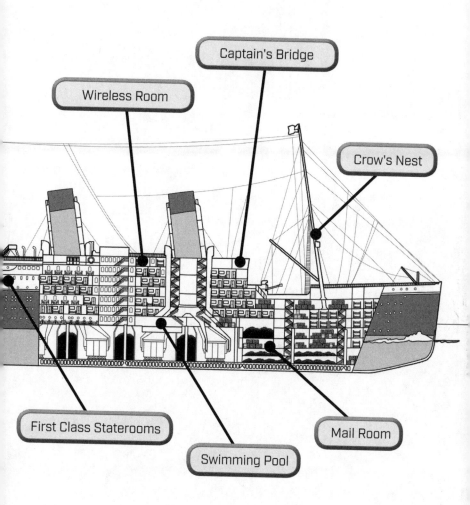

Captain's Bridge

Wireless Room

Crow's Nest

First Class Staterooms

Swimming Pool

Mail Room

CHAPTER ONE

PATRICK KELLEY

Tuesday, April 2, 1912;
Port of Belfast, Ireland

I'd heard that the *Titanic* was a grand ship. But the picture in my head vanishes when I actually see it. The *Titanic* is so much bigger! I stand on the dock staring at it. The ship is so huge, it's impossible to look at it all at once. It has rows of windows like a city block of houses. I can see decks full of tables and chairs, but they look like dollhouse furniture compared to the huge ship. The four smokestacks are taller than any building in my Irish village.

Those that built the ocean liner at the shipyard in Belfast often bragged about her. "The *Titanic* is the world's largest moving vessel!" they'd say. "She's the largest passenger steamship! The engines burn through six hundred and fifty tons of coal a day! And her three anchors weigh fifteen ton each!" They went on and on.

I see now that their boasts didn't exaggerate. It is like a floating city. There is a restaurant, fancy dining rooms, and luxury suites. The *Titanic* has enough room for some three-thousand, five-hundred souls, including hundreds of crew members. That is why I am boarding the *Titanic*. I am lucky enough to get one of these jobs. Not shoveling coal into boiler furnaces like my uncles on other ships. I am a bit small for thirteen and not strong enough for that type of work. No, my job is as a bellboy. Still, I will wear a White Star Line uniform and cap.

The man who hired me said I was the youngest employee on the *Titanic*. Well, at least on its maiden voyage to New York. He winked at me and said, "Not that anyone need know that, Mr. Kelley." I'm not going to test my luck. No one is going to learn that fact from me. Especially Father and Mother. They were against me signing on with White Star.

"You're too young, Patrick!" Mother pleaded. "The

wages aren't worth it. We'll get by." But I knew better. Without money coming in, my younger brother would have to do as I'd done and quit school at age twelve.

"Work will show up around here," Father argued. "You've no need to work on a ship." He seemed angry when he said it. But I saw fear in his face. His father was lost at sea years earlier.

"I'll be fine," I told them. "Our own countrymen built the *Titanic*. She's the safest ship yet. I'll be home in a month's time—no worse for wear."

REALITY CHECK

DID KIDS REALLY WORK ON SHIPS?

Absolutely. There were two fourteen-year-old boys working on the *Titanic*. One transferred from another ship, so it wasn't even his first job at sea. In 1912, only someone twelve or under was generally considered to be a child. Teenagers had all sorts of full-time jobs from servants and sailors to farmers and factory workers. Child labor laws in the United States wouldn't be passed until the 1930s.

CHAPTER TWO

SARAH WALSH

Thursday, April 11, 1912;
Port of Queenstown, Ireland

How am I supposed to find Uncle James on such a gigantic ship?

A man in a White Star uniform offers his hand to me as I climb the steep gangplank. "Welcome, miss, to the *Titanic's* maiden voyage," he says. "Aren't you lucky!"

I smile, but I won't feel lucky until I sit on my own bed in America with Puck licking my face and wagging his tail. Oh, to be off this moldy island and home in Boston! If I had a penny for every mention of luck during this past month in Ireland, I'd be rich! Then I'd get a first-class suite next to Dorothy Gibson. Maybe I'll see the film star. Now *that* would be lucky.

"Are you alone, miss?" asks the uniformed man.

"No, sir," I say. "I'm meeting my uncle, Mr. James Colvin, on deck."

He nods, then shouts overly loud, "All aboard for New York! Last call for New York!"

Following the crowd of passengers boarding the ship, I find myself up on the second-class deck. It's chilly, but not windy. The air smells of salt and smokestacks. I weave through people moving towards the deck's railing. The huge ship is picking up speed as it leaves port. The *Titanic* is underway at last.

I look around, wondering how to find my uncle among the mass of people on this huge ship. But it isn't difficult. There he is, near the far railing. I recognize his short-legged, big-bellied shape under his overcoat. "All Colvin men look ready to tip over," Mother always says.

Uncle is talking to a young steward taller than himself by a full head. I walk toward them.

"What's the girl look like?" asks the steward.

"I can't say," says Uncle. "I've not seen her in years. She's only a niece by marriage. I'm to see she gets on a train to Boston from New York. I'm a busy man, but family duty calls." I watch him scan the deck, looking past me twice!

He's not going to recognize me, is he? I'm nearly close enough to kick him.

"Hello, Uncle," I say, walking up to him. "It's me, Sarah Walsh."

"Ah! You're found," says Uncle, glancing at his pocket watch.

"That's a bit o' luck, sir! The young lady found you," says the steward.

"Luck, indeed," I mutter as the steward walks away.

"I trust your visit was pleasant, Sarah," says Uncle. He grabs my suitcase and motions for me to follow him.

"Not really, Uncle. Nana, my grandmother, is ill," I tell him.

"Yes, I heard. Better that she not return to Boston then. Wise decision. She no longer brings in money, right?" he asks.

"Nana's too old for a job, if that's what you mean," I

tell him. She's my father's mother, not a servant.

"Exactly. Best she stay in Ireland, then. Foreign immigrants are meant to work, not live off charity," Uncle scolds.

"Father says all Americans were foreigners once," I respond as we turned another corner. Gosh, this ship is a maze!

"A foreigner *would* say that," Uncle huffs, pulling out his pocket watch again. "Did you find Ireland enjoyable?"

"No, not really, Uncle." I feel a little bad saying it, but it is the truth. I did not enjoy my stay.

"Oh?" Uncle responds, seeming to hear me for the first time.

"It was horrible at Aunt Fiona's. They called me a 'spoiled Yank,' and we had to use an outhouse and pump our own water. If you wanted a bath, you had to heat water on the woodstove and fill a tub in the kitchen. Aunt fed us potatoes with a bit of greasy meat for supper. We ate lumpy porridge for breakfast every day. And my cousins don't like me. They'd leave to do chores before

I was up and never come back to fetch me. They'd play outside in the rain all day, too. Who wants to do that? And when Nana became ill, only I kept her company. And after all of that, she decided not to come home to Boston!"

"Hmm," Uncle snorts. We squeeze past a bellboy carrying three suitcases. Red hair sticks out from under his dark cap. Suddenly, Uncle stops to face me. "Sarah, let me tell you something."

"Yes, Uncle," I say. Have I been impolite? Sometimes I answer questions that people didn't really ask.

"The Irish are different from you and me," he says. "They have lower standards for cleanliness, order, education, and honesty."

"But my father was born in Ireland," I say. Not that anyone could tell, really. He lost his accent as a teenager in Boston. And he seemed clean enough to me.

"Yes, and to his credit, he's worked hard to rid himself of lazy, filthy Irish habits," Uncle says. "Marrying my wife's sister has made him a much better class of man.

I'll never understand why your mother allowed you to go to Ireland with that old biddy in the first place."

Uncle's words feel like a slap. I hated being in Ireland, but I love Nana fiercely. She'd lived with us in Boston my whole life. When I was feverish, she sat with me. Nana helped me bury my old cat, Socks, when he died. She always made a special cake for my birthday, too. Will I ever see her again?

I can feel my throat tighten. "Thank you, Uncle," I manage to say. "You're busy. I can get myself to the room."

"Good. I may still make my business meeting." He is already turning his back to me. "See you at supper."

In an instant, he is gone, and I am all alone on the *Titanic*.

REALITY CHECK

WERE IRISH IMMIGRANTS TREATED UNFAIRLY IN 1912 AMERICA?
In many places, they were. Landlords wouldn't rent to them and IRISH NEED NOT APPLY signs showed up in workplaces and job advertisements. Part of the discrimination was religious. Most Irish immigrants were Catholic in a time when most U.S. citizens were Protestant Christians. Poverty and famine drove 4.5 million people to immigrate from Ireland to America between 1820-1930.

CHAPTER THREE

PATRICK

Thursday, April 11, 1912; onboard *Titanic*

So I am filthy and lazy just because I am from Ireland? The ignorance of some people. What a pompous American that man was! And what a terrible thing to say about that girl's father. For the sake of heaven, she must've felt like a crumb of dirt on his shoe.

"Boy, you there!" calls an older man wearing a top hat. He's just stepping out of a stateroom door.

"Yes, sir?" I set down the three suitcases I'm carrying.

"Don't put those down! That's our baggage. Bring them in," says the man, disappearing into the room.

I check the cabin number against the baggage tags.

I enter, set the suitcases down, and pocket the coin the top-hatted man gives me. "Thank you, sir." One down, fifty more deliveries to go!

Heading back to the bellboy station, I see the girl again. The one with dark hair, light eyes, and a horrible uncle. She is wandering the hallway carrying a suitcase and wearing a frown of frustration.

"Is it help you're needing, miss?" I ask, straightening my White Star uniform and trying to stand taller. Best she know I am an official employee. Even if I am the youngest of the lot!

"Yes, Mr. Steward, sir," she responds. "Could you please tell me which way E-4 is?"

"I'm no steward, miss," I tell her. "Just a bellboy. But I'd be happy to show you to your cabin." I take the suitcase from her hand.

The girl walks alongside me as we wind our way through the hallways. "Aren't you a bit young to work on a ship?" she asks.

"I am old enough." I stop walking. "Here we are. Level E, stateroom four, miss," I say, knocking on the door.

"No one's there," the girl lets me know, staring at the shiny brass E-4.

I open the door for her and carry in the suitcase. A man's coat hangs from a hook and a large suitcase is already carefully stowed away. The room smells of shaving soap and hair oil. Her uncle must have boarded the ship before Ireland. "Do you need help finding family onboard?"

She isn't listening. The girl is too busy looking around. With a surprised smile, she takes in the room's niceties. Like most second-class staterooms, there are two beds and a combination washstand and dresser made of mahogany wood. A sparkling porcelain washbowl nestled under a chrome faucet is built right into the dresser. She walks over and tugs on a curtain that hangs from an overhead railing.

"The curtain separates the sleeping areas, miss," I explain. The girl's look of delight fades. "Is there something wrong?"

"I was just thinking about my nana," she says. "The ship we came to Ireland on together wasn't half as nice."

"So you're Irish, then?" I ask, knowing it isn't so.

"Oh, no. I'm American," the girl says as if I'd called her a thief. "My dad was born in Ireland. I just went with Nana to visit her family there."

"That'd be your family, too, right? And any daughter of an Irishman is Irish in my book!" I say with a grin. "Can I help you find your nana?"

"She's not onboard. Nana isn't well. She stayed in Ireland." The girl mumbles, "I do miss her."

"I'm sorry to hear that," I say. "My name is Patrick Kelley, by the way. Kelley with two es."

"Nice to meet you, Patrick. I'm Sarah," she says.

"My grandmother always makes my favorite cake on my birthday," I offer up. I feel bad for her. She's clearly sad.

"Mine, as well! Is it sponge cake with cream?" Sarah lights up.

"And raspberry jam," I declare.

"Nana uses strawberry, but raspberry would be good, too." Sarah smiles.

"I'll miss out on cake this birthday though, since I'm at sea." I frown.

"Is your birthday soon?" she asks. "Mine is Sunday."

"I'll turn fourteen on Sunday!" I exclaim. "What are the chances of that?"

"We have the same birthday!" Sarah shouts. "Oh, but I'll only be eleven."

"Not a thing wrong with eleven," I say with a wink. "My brother has been eleven for months now. He's not half as brave as you, though. I can't imagine him traveling on a ship across the ocean by himself."

"My uncle is onboard," Sarah reminds me, blushing a bit. "He lives in New York."

"You'll make friends on the ship," I say. Sarah doesn't look convinced but wears a brave face. If it were my brother, he'd be crying a puddle by now. He's a spoiled thing. "And anyway, we'll find a way to celebrate our birthdays on Sunday." I turn toward the cabin door as a man strides in—the unkind uncle. He seems out of breath and quite irritated.

"Where did you run off to?" he asks Sarah. "I came to find you a quarter of an hour ago and you weren't here."

"I got lost, Uncle," Sarah says, looking down at the tiled floor. "Patrick helped me find the room."

"It was no trouble, sir," I say, understanding the uncle doesn't want me here. "Nice to meet you, Miss Sarah. Good day to you both."

As he shuts the cabin door, I hear Sarah's uncle scolding her. "How does that boy know your name?" he barks. "I expect you to behave like a proper young lady. I have business onboard and no time to supervise activities with playmates. Now, get dressed for dinner. We're already late!"

My heart goes out to young Sarah. It's a shameful

man that treats family so poorly. As if his niece be a burden! Does he not know what it feels like to be so far from home and alone? As I wind my way back to the bellboy station, I vow to keep an eye out for Sarah. That girl deserves to have a bit of fun onboard the *Titanic*.

REALITY CHECK

DID ROOMS, FOOD, AND ENTERTAINMENT VARY BETWEEN CLASSES?

First-class tickets on the *Titanic* were at least ten times the price third-class passengers paid. Money brought those who had it luxury and services. As was common for the time, there were separate cabin, dining, socializing, and deck areas for passengers traveling in first, second, and third class. Each passenger class had different meals served on distinctive tableware, too. However, third-class passengers fared better on the newly built *Titanic* than most ships of its era. The lower levels were heated, the cabins kept clean, and passengers were served three meals a day.

CHAPTER FOUR

SARAH

Friday morning, April 12, 1912; onboard *Titanic*

The second-class dining room seems pretty first-class to me. It has oak panels on the wall, nice tablecloths, and plates with pretty blue flowers. Last night's dinner included lamb with sweet mint sauce, baked haddock, and curried chicken and rice. The meal's four courses ended with two kinds of dessert *and* ice cream! Like the furniture on the ship Nana and I took to Ireland, the tables and chairs are bolted to the floor. But these dining chairs have red leather seats that swivel, so you can get up from the table easily. If only Uncle would let me leave.

"May I be excused now, Uncle? I've finished my breakfast," I ask quickly. Uncle has stopped talking business with another passenger just long enough to take a sip of coffee.

"See that you are on time for dinner this evening." He waves me away.

"I will, Uncle. Thank you." I manage to get up from the table without knocking over a single fancy glass. *Whew!* Free at last to explore the ship.

Now, where is that library I've heard about? I weave through the crowded dining room, head up the stairs, and get on an elevator. Who knew ships had elevators? I find the second-class entrance to the deck . . . but no library.

"You lost again, Sarah?" I hear a muffled voice behind me. It's the bellboy Patrick from yesterday. He's carrying a tall stack of white, folded somethings.

"Hello, Patrick. I'm just getting to know the ship a bit," I tell him. Why do I blush when I lie? Might as well fess up. "Okay, I got lost trying to find the library."

"Happy to take you there, if you don't mind a stop on the way," he says. "Come on, these aprons are heavy."

I follow as Patrick takes some stairs then makes a turn and opens a door. It leads us to more stairs and the entrance to a huge kitchen. The brightly lit kitchen is warm and smells like baking bread and simmering soup.

"Good morning, young Patrick," says a tall woman dressed in a white work dress. She sets down a tray of what looks like tiny chickens.

"Feeding pigeons to first class tonight, Bess?" asks Patrick with a smirk. The tall cook puts her hands on her hips and grins.

"Stuffed pheasant is being served, though not to mouthy bellboys," she says playfully. She takes the aprons from his arms. "Who's your friend there?"

"I'm Sarah," I tell her. "Nice to meet you, ma'am."

"Call me Bess, Sarah," says the woman.

"Is mama-cat Jenny about?" asks Patrick. "I'm sure Sarah would love to see her wee kittens."

Kittens! "Oh yes, please!" Just the thought of holding something furry with paws makes me homesick.

"You've not heard, Patrick? Jenny left while we were still in port Tuesday. Took her kittens with her, too. Dockhands saw her carry them down the gangplank one by one. Jim didn't stop her neither," Bess says.

"Who's Jim?" I blurt out.

"Jim's a scullion, washes dishes and such," explains Patrick. "He welcomed Jenny into the kitchen when she showed up hungry and ripe with kits. Fed her and put out a crate to birth her brood in."

"Jim got off the ship," Bess informs us. "I saw him carrying his duffel heading for the stairs. Said if Jenny thought the ship was unsafe, he did, too. He tried to talk me into leaving, as well." Bess shrugs. "Said he'd never forgive himself if something happened to me."

"He was sweet on you, Bess." Patrick is trying to comfort her, I think. "What did you say to him?"

"Told him my husband would never forgive me if I came home without a paycheck." Bess bursts out a loud laugh at that.

Another cook and a man in a suit holding a clipboard

stroll into the kitchen. Bess turns her attention to them, giving us a quick goodbye nod.

"Best be on our way, Sarah," Patrick whispers. We leave the kitchen and head for the library. I can't stop thinking about Jenny taking her kittens off the *Titanic* one by one. She probably just didn't like how crowded it was getting as more passengers got onboard.

"Is Jim an Irishman?" I ask.

"The scullion? No, he's English. Why?" asks Patrick.

"Leaving a ship because a cat moved her kittens sounds like Irish superstition."

"And what do you mean by that?" I almost run into the back of him, he stops so quickly on the stairs. Are these the same stairs we took to get here?

"You know, little fairy people, four-leaf clovers, lucky this and unlucky that. All that superstitious Irish stuff," I explain, hearing Nana in my head.

"Not every person born in Ireland believes the same things, Sarah." Patrick sounds annoyed. "Are Americans all the same? And thinking you might die at sea isn't being superstitious. It's facing the facts. If you think that everyone who goes to sea comes home, you're not as smart as I thought."

So much for the cheerful bellboy of yesterday. I can feel my face starting to turn red. "Oh, really? Well, if you think the ship will sink, why are *you* still on it?" I snap.

"I didn't say that," Patrick answers. "But I've three uncles working on ships right now. And I worry for them, like they do for me. My own grandfather was lost at sea long before you and I were even born."

My face stings with shame and anger. Of course I know accidents happen. I'm not a baby. Who is he to lecture me! "Maybe I'll look up some tragic Irish shipwrecks in the library," I say spitefully.

"Be my guest. There's the library entrance just ahead. Try not to get lost between here and there." And before I can think of anything snippy to say, he's gone.

REALITY CHECK

WAS JENNY A REAL CAT?

Probably! There were reports of a cat named Jenny living on the *Titanic* who gave birth to kittens while in port at Southampton, England. Sailors encouraged cats accompanying them on ships. They were great mice hunters.

DID SOMEONE LEAVE THE SHIP BECAUSE OF JENNY?

Maybe. The story goes that one of the coal-shoveling workers left the *Titanic* when he saw Jenny the cat carry her kittens off.

CHAPTER FIVE

PATRICK

Friday afternoon, April 12, 1912; onboard *Titanic*

People can be so ignorant! Sarah's words from this morning—*all that superstitious Irish stuff*—still echo in my head. Not all Irish believe in fairies. And besides, all sorts of people are superstitious, not just the Irish. But I still feel bad about snapping at her.

"Patrick! Are you daydreaming, boy?" My boss pushes a stack of paper into my hands. "Deliver these messages to second class at once. Off with you."

"Right away, sir!" I jog off. Once I find the right room, I slide a message under the door. So many messages! What possible news is so important that it can't be sent in a regular letter?

"Patrick! I thought I'd never find you!" comes a voice from behind me. It's Sarah.

"Didn't know I was lost." I slip the last message under a door, not bothering to look up.

"I've been searching for you," she says, her face blushing red. "I want to apologize."

"Do you, then? I'm listening," I say, standing up.

"I'm sorry for what I said about Irish shipwrecks and superstitions," Sarah blurts out. "And I'm really sorry your grandfather died at sea. That's horrible."

She does look sorry. "And I'm sorry I spoke harshly," I tell her. And I mean it.

"Can we still be friends?" asks Sarah shyly. "And celebrate our birthdays?"

"Only two more days!" I smile. "Want to come with me to find some of my relatives who are passengers onboard?"

"I'd like to see more of the ship," she says. "I asked around for you in the kitchen, on deck, and in the library—everyone knows you!"

"Well, bellboys run errands all over the ship," I explain as we take the stairs down. "And the bellboys are kept really busy."

"I'd no idea the *Titanic* had so many lower levels," she says, skipping a bit to keep up. "It feels colder down here."

"The third-class passengers have their own cabins, dining salon, and lounge," I explain. "Many are moving to America, so they are kept separate because of the health inspection. If you're diseased or sick, they could send you back." I stop in front of a gate.

"What brings you into the belly of the boat, Patrick?" asks a uniformed man. He walks toward us on the other side of the gate. "Not many get fancy messages down here."

"Just an errand, Frank," I tell him, crossing my fingers behind me. Frank opens the gate for us with a smile.

"Welcome to steerage, miss," says Frank, shaking

Sarah's hand. His new uniform already smells like pipe smoke.

"Sarah, meet Frank." I introduce them. "Who knew you had manners, Frank!" The guard gives me a smirk and closes the gate behind us.

"Why did he call it steerage?" asks Sarah.

"Most ships put third-class passengers near the back where the noisy, mechanical steering parts are," I explain. Sarah doesn't miss much! She's getting an eyeful down here. Her head turns one way and then another as we walk past cabins with open doors. Inside are stacked-up bunk beds. Some have beds for four or six; a few sleep eight or ten passengers.

"Did you know the toilets down here flush automatically?" I ask. Sarah shakes her head. "It's for those unfamiliar with the workings of modern toilets."

"I doubt my Irish cousins know how to flush a toilet," Sarah says. "We used an outhouse at Aunt Fiona's."

"I'm sure they've real toilets at school." Why do

Americans always think Ireland is a century behind them? "And I doubt every American farmhouse has a fancy bathroom."

"I guess not," Sarah agrees. "But I wouldn't want to use an outhouse during the winter in Boston!"

"Fair point," I nod. We step into the lounge. It's a big, open area with benches, tables, and chairs. People are playing cards, reading, and chatting. Small kids chase each other around, laughing and smiling. I can tell Sarah is trying not to stare at the passengers from around the world dressed differently and speaking foreign languages. I'm busy looking around myself. Where did my cousins get to?

"Patrick! Patrick Kelley!" yells a young woman standing by a bench. It's cousin Mary! Her brother, Will, waves to me from her side. Sarah and I walk over and greet them. I make introductions all around.

"Mary and Will's mother is a cousin of my mother," I explain.

"My husband's already living in New York," says Mary, sitting down on the bench. "Will is going to work with him at the factory."

"Tell us about this grand ship, Patrick," says Will. "We don't see the fancy parts down here." I tell them about the first-class staterooms, the glass-domed grand staircase, and the dining hall with musicians and ladies in gowns.

"Have you seen the film star Dorothy Gibson?" Sarah blurts out. Her eyes are so wide they look like giant marbles.

"No, but the housekeeper says she has ten gowns and three furs," I tell her. Mary seems impressed by this, though not Will.

"Tell them about Jenny the cat and scullion Jim!" Sarah demands. So I do, and Will soaks up every word.

"Being at sea doesn't frighten you, Patrick?" asks Will.

"I've got my Saint Christopher." I pull the chain out

from under my collar. The silvery medal shines as it dangles.

Mary picks up her handiwork, saying, "May the patron saint of travelers keep us safe, cousin."

I glance over at Sarah. Does she think this is another silly Irish superstition? But she seems more interested in what Mary is crocheting.

"I need to get back to work now," I let them know. Hopefully, no one has missed me.

"You're welcome to spend the afternoon with us, Sarah," says Mary.

"I'd like that," Sarah says, moving closer to sit by Mary. "Your crocheting is beautiful." Sarah seems comfortable here. No harm letting her stay, I think. The company will do her good.

"The guard, Frank, will let you pass when you leave," I tell Sarah. "I'll remind him." Then I say my goodbyes.

As I turn to leave, Will joins in with a nearby group singing. Their voices echo as I make my way up and out of steerage. *But come ye back when summer's in the meadow.* . . . The song is my father's favorite. I wonder if he is still angry that I left? I hope not.

REALITY CHECK

Why would people think a ship is unsinkable?

The *Titanic* had a high-tech (for its time) safety feature. The part of the ship that sat below the water was divided up into sixteen compartments. Watertight steel doors separated each to prevent any flooding water from spreading. The ship was designed to stay afloat even if four compartments filled up with water.

CHAPTER SIX

SARAH

Saturday, April 13, 1912; onboard *Titanic*

Uncle James doesn't even look up from his eggs when I ask to be excused from the breakfast table. I am up and away in a dash, skipping down the hallway. *Will I be able to get back into the third-class lounge by myself*, I wonder. Mary promised to show me that special crocheting she does. And Will said he'd teach me some songs that Father will remember from Ireland. If that same guard is there, will he remember me?

"Good morning, Sarah!" I hear the now-familiar, cheery voice behind me. Patrick! "How'd you like a look inside a film star's fancy first-class cabin?"

"Dorothy Gibson's room!" I nearly scream.

"Shhh. The housekeeper told me Miss Gibson will be

at the beauty salon for an hour. Come on! Let's have a quick peek!" Patrick can't help but grin.

We weave our way up and over to the first-class suites. Looking around, Patrick quietly pulls open a door and peeks inside. "Be quick, now!" he whispers.

We slip inside, shutting the door behind us. The suite is a palace! Colorful silk curtains cover a big window. Through the thick glass is a view of endless steel-gray water and sky. There is a living room with a sofa, woven rug, and low table. The remains of breakfast served on gold-rimmed china sit on a silver tray. There is even an attached bathroom with a tub! It smells of perfumed soaps and creams. A wardrobe door is ajar, and inside I can see sparkly gowns and fur coats—and at least six hatboxes!

"We best go, Sarah," urges Patrick. There are muffled sounds in the hallway. Oh, no! Getting caught in here will land Patrick in a lot of trouble. I can't even imagine what Uncle would say.

I crack open the door just enough to look out. "It's

clear!" I say, stepping out into the hallway. Patrick follows right behind me, closing the door. We quickly make our way down the hallway.

"Patrick! Why are you up here? There are messages waiting to be delivered," scolds a stern-looking man.

"On my way there now, sir," Patrick replies. "Just helping this young lady find her way."

"It's such a big ship!" I cry, trying to look lost.

"Indeed," says the man, looking at Patrick. "Off with you both. And no lollygagging!"

Our steps are brisk until we turn a corner. I take one look at Patrick, and we both burst out laughing. "Whew!" I say, trying to catch my breath and slow my pounding heart. "That was close!"

"It was worth it! What a room, huh?" Patrick shakes his head. "I'd like to buy first-class tickets for Mother and Father someday. Not on the *Titanic*, necessarily. Perhaps on a ship to London."

"They'd love that, I'm sure," I say. Patrick looks deep in thought. "You better pick up those messages, Patrick."

"Right you are." He perks up. "Mary and Will hoped you'd come back down today, by the way."

"Can I get back into third-class?" I ask hopefully.

"Frank the guard is on duty. He'll let you in," Patrick tells me. "Tell my cousins hello." And just like that, he is gone with a wave.

Frank opens the gate for me without a second look. And I find Mary and Will among the familiar benches and tables. The lounge is full of people playing cards, kids making up games, and people talking in different languages. I like it here. It's exciting.

"It's coming along nicely, Sarah," says Mary. She studies the lace I am crocheting. "You've learnt quickly!"

"Mother taught me to crochet doilies," I explain. "But these patterns are more complicated." I am copying a lacy shawl Mary wears. Inside each square is a swirly shape made from chains of crocketed lace thread. The chains weave in and out, forming stars, triangles, and rosettes. If you trace a chain as it loops, you can't tell where it starts or ends.

"Those are Celtic knots, Sarah," says Will. "They go on forever. That's what makes them special."

"And take me forever to make, too," laughs Mary. "How about another song, Will? Entertain us while we crochet eternity."

The three of us pass the afternoon singing and crocheting. Mary helps me make a Celtic knot. It is a bit uneven, in truth. And I try to remember the words to the songs so I can write them down later. I tell Patrick's cousins about sneaking into Dorothy Gibson's room. Mary asks me to describe the gold-rimmed dishes twice. "Who needs six different hats on a boat?" jokes Will.

Will has lots of questions about America. He seems worried about finding a job in New York. "Is it true the Irish are unwelcome there?" he asks.

"I don't really know, Will. I've never been to New York," I say. What's the point in worrying him? I promise to give him my address. Perhaps Father would have some advice for him. I wonder how Father felt leaving Ireland.

Why have I never asked him? A wave of homesickness washes over me. I've never had a birthday without family. Uncle James does *not* count.

The thought reminds me of something. "Tomorrow is Patrick's birthday," I say. "We should surprise him—with a cake. A sponge one with cream and raspberry jam. The kind his grandmother makes him."

"A lovely thought, Sarah," Mary says. "But how can we make a cake here?"

"I'll think of something," I promise. "But don't tell him. It should be a surprise." Surely there is a sponge cake somewhere on the *Titanic*!

REALITY CHECK

WAS DOROTHY GIBSON A REAL FILM STAR?
Yes! She starred in dozens of silent films and was among the highest-paid movie actresses of her time. Gibson wasn't the only famous *Titanic* passenger. A number of multimillionaires, wealthy socialites, and members of the British aristrocracy, including the Countess of Rothes, were onboard.

CHAPTER SEVEN

PATRICK

Saturday evening, April 13, 1912; onboard *Titanic*

"Don't say anything, alright? It should be a surprise," I say. My cousins nod.

"Sarah will be pleased." Mary smiles. "Turning eleven so far from home can't be easy."

"She's learned quite a few Irish songs, too!" says Will. We laugh at that. Will would teach songs to a cat if he could.

"Good evening to you all," I say. "There's messages waiting for me to deliver." We exchange goodbyes and I begin to weave through a crowd of passengers trying to pass the time on my way to the gate.

Outside the busy, second-class dining room, I spot Sarah. She is with her grouchy uncle. I can hear his booming voice from here. "I'm going to the smoking room to talk business, Sarah. I expect you to go directly back to the cabin," he says. Why does his voice always sound so mean-spirited?

Sarah says something, nods, and waits for her uncle to leave. Then she walks in the opposite direction of her cabin and nearly crashes into me.

"Oh! Hello, Patrick," Sarah greets me.

"What are you up to?" I ask with a grin.

"I'm going outside. Up on the deck," she says excitedly. "A woman at our dinner table said there are a million stars in the sky tonight."

"Near the crow's nest would be good," I tell her. "It's where the lookouts climb up and watch the water, away from lights on the ship."

"Perfect! It'll be extra-dark there," Sarah says. "Can you show me where it is?"

"Sure! I'm done working for tonight—more or less," I say. "The crow's nest is in the front of the ship."

"The bow, right?" asks Sarah.

"Aren't you a quick study!" I'm impressed. We head toward the front of the *Titanic*, open a door, and step outside near the ship's bridge. The air is sharp and cold.

"That's where Captain Smith steers the ship, right?" asks Sarah, rubbing her arms. She points toward the bridge's line of windows.

"He gives the orders. But someone else turns the wheel," I explain. At least that's what I'd heard. Captain Smith doesn't talk to bellboys.

"Look up!" Sarah points to the sky. And I do. With no moon or clouds, the stars are like a shimmering blanket.

"There are so many!" Sarah is in awe. "It's hard to make out any constellations." She's right. Even the stars above the dark Irish countryside aren't so bright. My little brother and I used to climb up on the roof and stargaze. I wonder if he still went up on the roof alone now that I'm gone.

"It's hard to see stars in Boston. I can't wait to tell Father about this," Sarah says. "And the Irish songs Will taught me. Mother won't believe my crocheting, either."

"Glad you're finally having a good time," I say. "Your Irish cousins should see you now!"

"I should've tried harder to have fun with them. Ireland *was* pretty," Sarah said. "I am a spoiled Yank in some ways, I guess. It's not Aunt Fiona's fault they don't have much money."

"Your nana got sick, though. That was difficult." I don't want her to be so hard on herself. It can't be easy visiting a new place with different ways. I'm lost in thought when Sarah hands me a slip of paper. It is an address in Boston, Massachusetts.

"I wrote this down for Will. But I'll write it down again for him later," Sarah says. "Maybe we could be pen pals."

"What a grand idea! I'll write my home address down for you tomorrow," I say. An American pen pal! I'd have to practice my penmanship.

"Hey, look! They're changing lookouts," I say, pointing. Sarah lifts her eyes toward the crow's nest. It looks like a tall metal tub attached to the mast. One man is climbing up. When he reaches the bottom of the crow's nest, he opens a hatch and pops up inside it. Over his head hangs a bell. Then the other lookout starts to climb down.

"How can he see anything out there in the dark?" Sarah asks. The air is still and the sea glassy calm. No moon and an ink-black sky. I can't see that far at all.

The off-duty lookout isn't far from us on deck. "Did you spot any icebergs, sir?" I yell.

"Aye. You feel the deep cold of the air, lad?" he asks. "A sure sign that ice is out there."

"How many icebergs did you see, sir?" asks Sarah.

"A half dozen or so, off in the distance," the lookout tells us. "It's hard spotting 'em without the binoculars." And with that, he turns and takes some stairs up toward the bridge.

"So it's true then," I mutter.

"What's true?" asks Sarah.

"Something a steward told me," I say. "That the binoculars are kept in a locker, and the locker's key got left in England by mistake." Without binoculars, a lookout won't see an iceberg until it is pretty close. Would that leave enough time to turn the *Titanic* away from it?

"Someone's in trouble for that!" Sarah huffs, rubbing her arms again. "It is 'deep cold' out here. Let's go inside."

"Yes!" I say. "Lookout is too cold of a job for me." My breath is like smoke from a woodstove. So much responsibility, too. Imagine how you'd feel if an iceberg hit the ship because you hadn't spotted it in time? We head for the door. Warmth and light greet us on the other side.

REALITY CHECK

Were binoculars really not used because they were locked away?

Yes! An officer named David Blair was replaced at the last minute. He mistakenly took the locker key with him when he left the ship. The *Titanic* hit the iceberg only 37 seconds after the lookout spotted it and rang the bell. The ship started to turn, but there wasn't enough time to avoid hitting the iceberg. The lookout would have likely spotted the iceberg sooner if he'd had binoculars. That extra time might have been enough to avoid collision.

CHAPTER EIGHT

SARAH

Sunday morning, April 14, 1912; onboard *Titanic*

My eyes open. I'm eleven! Finally, eleven. Happy birthday to me! I get up and notice that Uncle James has already left. I don't think he could have given me a better gift. Maybe having a birthday on a ship in the middle of the ocean isn't so bad after all.

When I get to breakfast, Uncle James is waiting for me. "There you are, Sarah," he says. "I attended church services this morning. Being a Catholic, you wouldn't have been welcome."

"Good morning, Uncle," I respond, feeling my face flush. "Thank you for being considerate," I say through clenched teeth. Why must he make every sentence a criticism? Everyone else at the table seems suddenly busy. Toast is buttered, cream poured into coffee. I slide into my swiveling chair.

An elderly gentleman breaks the silence. "I took a quick stroll on the deck earlier," he announces. "My, it's turned cold! They say we've entered an ice field."

"An ice field! If icebergs are about, shouldn't the ship slow its speed?" gasps a woman wearing a green dress.

"Captain Smith will have none of that," remarks Uncle James. "This is the *Titanic's* maiden voyage! She must arrive on time in New York. It's full speed ahead down below."

I hope he is wrong. Isn't it better to be safe and a bit late? After finishing breakfast, I make my way down to the kitchen. I have a plan for getting Patrick a birthday cake—and her name is Bess.

"It's a perfect surprise!" Bess croons. "And a wee cake is no trouble at all." The kitchen smells of roast beef today.

"Thank you, Bess!" I say. "Patrick's been such a

good friend to me. I wanted to do something nice for his birthday."

"Young Patrick's a kind lad. I'm happy to help," she responds.

The surprise plan might just work! Bess will make a small cake for Patrick. She'll get it to Frank, the guard. Then I'll pick it up on my way into third class after dinner tonight. Hopefully, no one will blab! I can't wait to tell Mary and Will!

I leave the busy kitchen and start walking toward the ship's stern. People are strolling about dressed in their Sunday best. Laughter drifts by from a group of men playing cards. At the gate into third class, I catch Frank up on the plan. I explain that a kitchen worker will deliver the cake. I remind him that it is a surprise.

"I'll take good care of the cake, Miss Sarah," Frank assures me. He opens the gate to let me into third class. "And my lips are sealed!"

The lounge seems quieter today. Is it because it's Sunday? Or because it is extra-chilly in here? I walk by a row of small, round windows. The sea outside is frigid and gray, but still calm. Chunks of ice float here and there. But none are bigger than a crate.

"Good morning, Sarah!" calls a friendly voice. It's Will. "Hope you dressed warm enough for third class," he says with a smile. I follow him over to where Mary is sitting, a blanket across her lap. I tell them the details of Patrick's surprise birthday cake.

"Can't wait to see the look on Patrick's face!" Will grins. The cousins seem pleased with the plan and agree to their part: Get Patrick down to third class tonight.

"Scoot in next to me, Sarah," Mary says. She refolds the blanket so it covers my lap as well. "Let's see your lacework." I run my fingers over the plain white cord.

The afternoon passes like the day before. Will sings and teaches me songs. Mary helps me practice crocheting never-ending Celtic knots. All around us, people fill their time with games and stories, naps and songs. I overhear immigrants trading advice on finding work and rooms to rent. They plan for what's next with nervous hope. Somehow, I feel at home here. At home! In a room full of strangers on a ship in the middle of the ocean? How is that possible?

When dinnertime comes around, I leave third class. "Uncle is expecting me," I tell Mary and Will. "I'll be back later—for the surprise!" Frank lets me through the gate. The metal feels like ice. He puts his finger to his lips with a wink.

Back on the upper levels, I head toward our cabin. Uncle James isn't there, so I quickly change clothes. I don't want him scolding me for being late.

As I hurry to the second-class dining room, I hear someone call my name. "Sarah! Over here!" It's Patrick. He's slipping messages under doors. "Happy birthday to us!" he says. "Remember?"

"Oh, right!" I try to act like I've forgotten. "Happy birthday, Patrick!"

"Many happy returns to you, too," he says.

What luck running into Patrick! This will help the plan. "I visited Will and Mary today," I tell him. "They want you to go see them after supper."

"Is everything all right?" Patrick asks.

"Oh, yes," I say, trying to think fast. "Um, some kind of family news. Just make sure to go down there later tonight."

"Will do. Thanks, Sarah." Patrick looks determined. "You're dressed for dinner, I see. And I'm off to the wireless room. The telegraph messages keep coming in!"

The telegraph. Would Mother and Father have sent me a birthday telegraph? "Do you think I could have a message waiting?" I ask shyly.

"I suppose you might," Patrick says. Then he smiles, seeming to understand. "We should definitely check."

The wireless is a cramped room filled with machines. The operator is sitting at a desk, hunched over. The young man writes with one hand and has a receiver over an ear. There is paper everywhere. Stacks of it. People keep buzzing in and out of the tiny room, too.

Some drop off sheets of paper. Others pick some up. How does anyone keep track of it all!

"Here are the passenger messages," Patrick says, pointing to a pile.

"Shhh," growls the operator. He points to a sign that reads: QUIET PLEASE.

Patrick quickly gathers up all the papers from a particular pile. The top one slips off. When I kneel to pick it up, I see another message on the floor.

"Patrick, this . . ." I say.

"Shhh!" hisses the operator. He looks at Patrick and points to the door. His message is crystal clear: Out! Patrick grabs my arm and we leave the room.

"Patrick, I'm sorry!" I exclaim. "But look at this message!"

Date: April 14, 1912   Time: 1:45 pm
To: RMS Titanic
From: SS Amerika

Message: Passed two large icebergs near your route.

"You're right, Sarah. This is important!" Patrick grabs the message and heads back into the wireless room.

I suddenly feel frightened standing alone on this massive ship in the middle of the freezing ocean. I wring my hands until Patrick reappears. "I left it under the operator's nose. He'll pass it onto Captain Smith."

Patrick notices my fear and tries to reassure me. "Don't worry, Sarah. I know all of this may seem a bit hectic, but icebergs are common out here."

I feel better knowing Patrick is not scared. "Thanks, Patrick. You're a good friend," I tell him. "Well, if there's no telegraph from my parents, I better get to the dining room." It hardly seems important now when compared to iceberg reports.

"Afraid not," Patrick says. He shuffles through the stack of messages a second time. "Maybe one will come in tomorrow."

"It's all right," I say, walking toward second class.

"Bye! Don't forget to go see Mary and Will later." Patrick waves and rounds a corner.

Dinner is endless. It's like one of those Celtic knots I've been crocheting. The adults never stop talking as plates, cups, bowls, and glasses are brought and taken away. I'm in agony waiting for dinner to finish so I can pretend to go to sleep! Then I plan on sneaking out and going down to Patrick's surprise in third class. Frank probably has the cake by now. The thought makes me grin.

"Sarah!" snaps Uncle James. "Mrs. Cooper just asked you a question."

"How was your day, dear?" repeats Mrs. Cooper. She reminds me of a teacher.

"It was interesting, ma'am. I found out there are large icebergs nearby," I report. Then I tell her about the message from the nearby ship. I leave out how I saw the message, though. I don't want to risk getting Patrick in trouble.

"Young ladies don't spread gossip and rumors, Sarah," Uncle scolds me. "Please excuse my niece's bad manners."

"Even so, dear, there's no need to worry," says Mrs. Cooper. "We're onboard the world's safest ship with White Star's best captain."

"It is a state-of-the-art vessel," agrees Uncle James.

"They call Captain Smith the millionaires' captain, you know," continues the woman. "Many of these rich and famous passengers refuse to travel with any other captain. Aren't we lucky to be onboard the *Titanic* with them?"

"Yes, ma'am," I politely answer. But I don't feel lucky when I imagine the *Titanic* weaving around icebergs in the dark.

REALITY CHECK

DID THE TELEGRAPH OPERATOR REALLY IGNORE ICEBERG WARNINGS? Iceberg alerts started coming in on the morning of April 14, 1912. Warnings continued all day. One from a German ocean liner, the *Amerika*, was never passed onto the bridge. The actual message read: *Amerika passed two large icebergs [at] 41° 27° N, 50° 8' W on April 14*. Regardless, the captain was aware of the iceberg warnings. Still, he never slowed the ship in response to them. The *Titanic* continued on full speed ahead through the ice field.

CHAPTER NINE

PATRICK

Sunday night, April 14, 1912; onboard *Titanic*

Turning a corner, I start down the last set of stairs. What a day this has been! *Take this here, Patrick. . . . Go run this over there, Patrick. . . . There are more messages to deliver, Patrick. . . .* Being a bellboy is hard work. But still, it's nothing like shoveling coal into furnaces down in the ship's belly. And the wages are twice what I made running errands for shopkeepers back home.

I am almost to the third-class gate. Hopefully, Will and Mary were successful with my plan. They promised to trick Sarah into coming down to third class tonight. I wonder how they did it. Or if they did. I was confused by Sarah saying they wanted to see *me*. I guess it's likely part of whatever scheme they've invented. She is going to be so surprised!

"Still on duty, Frank?" I ask the guard. He opens the gate and lets me pass.

"Here all night tonight," says Frank with a sly smile. "Napped at dinnertime."

"Glad to hear it," I say with a wave.

Will, Mary, and Sarah aren't hard to find. When I walk into the lounge, it's mostly empty. The three of them are over in a corner standing around a little table.

As I walk up to them, they all turn around and yell, "Surprise!" On the table stands a very lovely cake.

"Happy birthday, cousin!" says Will, reaching out to shake my hand.

"Many happy returns, Patrick!" calls out Mary. She hugs me hard.

Everyone turns to me and laughs. I must seem stunned.

Sarah looks proud. "I'm so glad our surprise worked! Bess made the cake."

"It's a sponge cake like my grandmother makes," I say, after taking a huge bite. It has cream and jam between the layers—raspberry! I can't believe it! My throat feels tight, and my eyes blink. "Thank you very much." I don't know what else to say.

The cake is incredibly delicious! Maybe as good as Grandmother's—not that I'd ever tell her that. The four of us eat every last crumb.

"I've a present for you," Sarah says, blushing. Then she hands me a neatly folded handkerchief. It's made by crochet in the Irish lace style. In its center is a large, intertwining design.

"It's the handsomest handkerchief I've ever laid eyes on," I tell her. It's the truth, too.

"That's a Celtic knot in the center," Sarah says, still blushing.

"Aren't you the pride of Ireland!" I tease.

"Not everything Irish is bad," she teases back. We all laugh at that.

"Now I've a birthday surprise for you, Sarah," I tell her.

"Really?" Sarah asks. She glances at Will and Mary, who look completely unsurprised.

"Come with me! Let's go!" Sarah and I hurry out of third class, moving forward through the ship, but staying on lower levels.

"Where are we?" asks Sarah, looking around. It is so quiet this late at night. There aren't many people about.

"You'll see," I say. We pass by a young man in uniform guarding a door. I talk with him for a minute, trying to keep my voice down.

"Half an hour, no more!" he says. Then we go inside.

With her first glance, I hear Sarah cry out, "A swimming pool! A real swimming pool!"

We quickly find swimming outfits in the lockers and get changed. I jump in with a big splash. The water is warm! Our laughter and my splashing echo in the pool room.

I swim back and forth across the pool three times without stopping. I'm showing off a bit. What a fun birthday! So much better than I expected.

"Are you not getting in, Sarah?" I ask. She sits on the pool edge splashing the water with her feet. "Can't you swim?" *Where do kids in a big city like Boston swim,* I wonder.

"I've never tried," she says.

"There's nothing to it!" I tell her. "You just make circles with your arms and kick your legs." I show her what I mean. Then I swim a lap to demonstrate. When I reach the end of the pool where she sits, Sarah is making circles in the air with her arms and kicking her legs. "That's great! Now all you need is water."

As I reach my hand out to help her into the pool, it suddenly feels like someone is pulling me under water. I kick my feet and turn around in time to see a wave of water pass through the pool. It sloshes up the side, soaking Sarah to her chin. As it breaks, I'm pulled away from the edge and have to kick even harder to keep from being pulled under. The lights flicker off and then back on. And then it's quiet. Too quiet.

"The engines have stopped," I say quietly, almost whispering. Something is terribly wrong. We quickly find dry towels, change clothes, and leave the pool. It's nearly midnight. "You best go back to your cabin, Sarah." My boss told us to report to the bellboy station if anything unusual happens. Does this count? On our way up from the pool, we hear shouting and running. Following the noise, Sarah and I come out onto an outside deck.

"This way, throw it here!" yells a boy. "I got you!" screams another. They are tossing and kicking around chunks of ice. They're laughing and running, sliding and slipping in the ice that's now all over the deck. *Where did all this ice come from*, I wonder.

"We hit an iceberg!" Sarah exclaims as she runs towards me. "That's what everyone is saying!" An iceberg! That explains the jolt I felt in the pool.

"I'm going to the bellboy station," I tell Sarah. "Come on." And we hurry back inside and wind our way through the hallways.

"No one seems worried," says Sarah. "The iceberg must not have hurt the ship."

"Maybe not," I say. "But the engines aren't back on yet." I can't imagine how you look for damage on such a huge ship. Especially at night and in the middle of the ocean. As we turn a corner, we see two postal clerks coming our way. Both men are wet up to their hips. Each carry a duffel bag of mail on his shoulder.

"Have you come from the mail room?" I ask. The storage room for mail is on level G, which is windowless, below the water line, and nearby one of the engine rooms.

"Aye, laddie, we have," says the older man with a Scottish accent. "She's flooded down there. We're getting out what mail we can."

"Flooded! With seawater?" gasps Sarah. She looks as pale as marble.

"Aye. Not a pretty sight. Envelopes and packets floating around. Most of them ruined likely," he says. Who cares about wet letters and packages? The ship is flooding!

The Scotsman takes note of our shocked faces. "No need to fret," he says calmly. "Nearby ships are surely on their way already. Everyone will be off before a foot gets damp." He waves as he passes us in the hallway. The other postal clerk says nothing and never looks up. I can't get him to meet my glance.

REALITY CHECK

Did the iceberg rip a hole in the Titanic?

Not exactly. The right front side of the ship scraped against the iceberg, shaving off the heads of rivets that held the hull's steel plates together. Those plates pulled apart, unzipping a section of the ship's hull as long as long as a football field. Seven tons of seawater per second began flooding in.

Did the mail room really flood?

Yes! The Royal Mail Ship, or RMS, *Titanic* carried more than 3,350 bags of mail. The post office, or mail room, where it was sorted and stored was in the bow of the ship deep down on level G.

CHAPTER TEN

SARAH

Monday, April 15; 12:30 am
onboard *Titanic*

I don't believe that Scottish mail clerk. He talked to us in that way grown-ups do when they think you're too young to understand something. And that younger mail clerk looked so scared. What had he seen? Their feet looked plenty damp already to me. Patrick will find out what is going on from the other bellboys soon, but I need to warn Uncle James.

When I get to our cabin, he is snoring loudly. Uncle slept through the iceberg crash! I go ahead and change into my warmest clothes and put on my wool coat. Then I find the life vests under the bed. I pull back the curtain that divides the room.

"Uncle! Wake up!" I yell, shaking his shoulders. "We've hit an iceberg!" I put my life vest on, tying it tightly. "We need to be ready to leave the ship." His eyes open and he stares at me.

"What's the meaning of this, Sarah! Why are you out of bed?" he yells.

I tell him about the ice on the deck and the flooded mail room, but he doesn't listen, he is too furious. "I *forbade* you from leaving this room after dinner! Running wild through the ship with Irish workers! How could you embarrass me like this! After all I've done for you!"

"I'm sorry, Uncle," I say. How can I make him understand? "The ship is going to sink, Uncle," I tell him. "Get dressed and put on your life vest."

"I'll do no such thing. What foolish Irish tales of icebergs have filled your head? You get back in bed this instant, young lady. I'm confining you to this room until we reach New York."

"Uncle, it's true! We hit an iceberg! You were asleep when it happened! Can't you hear the difference? The engines are off!"

A brisk knock at the door stops our argument. A sleepy-looking steward stands outside the cabin door. People are shuffling by behind him. They wear coats and life vests. "Sir, miss. Pardon the interruption," he says. "Passengers are asked to move to the decks. Immediately."

"Whatever for, young man?" Uncle asks.

"Rescue ships have been alerted, sir," said the steward. "The *Titanic* is taking on water."

"Taking on water?" asks Uncle. "What the devil is going on?" His irritation finally shifts to panic.

"We hit an iceberg, sir," explains the steward. "Now please do as the captain has asked."

"Captain Smith?" Uncle asks in confusion. I can't wait any longer. We're all in danger and Uncle is not being any help. If the *Titanic* is taking on water, there is no way I'm going to sit locked in my room waiting for seawater to pour in. I need to find Patrick. He'll know what is happening. I toss the other life vest at Uncle James and sprint out of the cabin. "Sarah! Come back here!" I hear him yell as I run down the hallway.

I push my way past the crowd. Passengers are slowly heading outside. Little kids rub their eyes. Pajamas peek out beneath their coats. When I finally reach the deck, the frigid outside air hits me like a slap. The black sky overhead is like a dome that ends at the smooth, dark water. Ocean surrounds us as far as I can see. I look in every direction. There isn't a ship anywhere. Not a speck of light except the stars overhead. Where are the rescue ships?

All over the deck, uniformed men are turning over lifeboats. One lifeboat is already upright and hanging over the ship's edge. It was mostly empty, but a few people are climbing into it. One is Dorothy Gibson! The film star looks nervous, but still glamorous. Her hands grab the seat beneath her tightly as the boat sways on its ropes a bit. It looks scary hanging from ropes far above the sea. Miss Gibson gasps when the ropes begin to move. Why are they lowering the lifeboat with only a dozen people in it?

"Don't launch it yet!" I yell. "There's room for five times as many people on that boat!" I can feel a sudden slant in the deck. It's like standing on a ramp. A horrible realization washes over me. It's true. We are sinking. Why aren't more people getting into lifeboats?

"This way, miss. Not to worry," coaxes a deckhand. "Plenty of room for you in that boat over there." He points across the deck at another lifeboat. "Women and children!" he yells. Another deckhand is putting children and women in a lifeboat first, but then letting men in, too. The evacuation seems as unorganized as the wireless room was.

Where is everyone? And why aren't more people getting into boats? Clusters of passengers stand around whispering, watching with wide eyes at the swaying lifeboats being lowered. Others look down at the small lifeboats rowing away from the huge ship in the dark, cold sea below. They feel safer here. And why shouldn't they? They've just come from their beds. They haven't seen any flooding. Most look to be first-class passengers from the upper levels. And then a new panic hits me. Where are all the third-class passengers?

REALITY CHECK

DID THE CREW PRACTICE EVACUATION MANEUVERS?
They were supposed to, but had not. The crew ran out of time before the *Titanic* launched. Captain Smith canceled a lifeboat drill the morning of April 12th, just days before the *Titanic* would sink.

WERE THE LIFEBOATS FILLED TO CAPACITY?
No. Many were launched half filled at best. At the beginning, people were reluctant to get in the boats. Once no other women or children were waiting for a particular boat, it was lowered so the next one could be filled. As panic set in, the boats became fuller, but without proper training, some of the deckhands didn't know how many people each boat would hold. When one looked full, they simply launched it without counting.

CHAPTER ELEVEN

PATRICK

Monday, April 15; 1:20 am
onboard *Titanic*

The *Titanic* is sinking. Boss doesn't sugarcoat it. He tells us rescue ships are coming, but the nearest one, called *Carpathia,* is more than a couple of hours away. His last orders to us bellboys are, "Stay out of the deckhands' way. There aren't enough lifeboats. None of you will get a place on one." If it comes to it, we are expected to go down with the ship.

Not enough lifeboats! I need to tell Sarah. I make a dash for the deck, figuring maybe she is already outside. Then I see her sprinting down the stairs. "Sarah!" I yell, running to catch her. "Sarah, turn around! You need to get in a lifeboat. There aren't enough for everyone."

"Oh, no! And they're launching them half full, too!" she tells me.

"The ship is truly sinking, Sarah. Get in a lifeboat!" I beg.

"I will," she says. "But there aren't any third-class passengers on the deck. We need to find . . ."

"Mary and Will!" I gasp. More than half of the ship's passengers are third-class. Why aren't they up on the deck yet? "I'll find my cousins, Sarah. Get in a lifeboat. NOW!"

I leave Sarah standing there, then turn and push my way through the thick stream of passengers heading for the deck. All of the lifeboats would be launched very soon.

The ship is really tilting now. I see water sloshing in the lower stairways as I run toward the gate. It seems like the ocean is completely inside the ship. I hear the third-class level before I see it. Passengers are yelling, kids are crying, and a familiar voice echoes in the dim hallway.

"This gate must remain closed! Take the exit up to the third-class deck! You can't go this way!" yells Frank. Passengers plead with him to let them through.

"Frank! The ship is sinking!" I shout. "There aren't lifeboats on the third-class deck. And that exit is already underwater. I just passed by it. You've got to open the gate! These people are trapped! It's going to flood down here."

"Sinking! How's that possible?" Frank is shocked and confused. At that moment, three large men push their way through the crowd of third-class passengers.

"Stand back!" yells one. Then they start kicking the gate. With their combined blows, they manage to break it open. Within seconds, people stream out and head for the stairs. I run against the flow, straight into third class.

"Mary! Will!" I cry out. "It's Patrick!" But they aren't in their cabin. Water is already covering half of the lounge floor. I wade in up to my knees and the water feels like pins stabbing me. The table my birthday cake sat on two hours ago floats by. I have to get out of here. Mary and Will must have gotten through the other exit before it flooded. I grab and kiss the St. Christopher medal hanging around my neck. Please keep them safe.

REALITY CHECK

WERE NEARBY SHIPS CALLED IN TO HELP?

The *Californian* was only two hours away, but had turned her radio off for the night after stopping because of the iceberg danger. And after sending the *Titanic* repeated ice warnings.

CHAPTER TWELVE

SARAH

Monday, April 15; 1:40 am
onboard *Titanic*

I can't get in a lifeboat without going back for Uncle James. The guilt would be too great. I just need a few minutes! But what if he still doesn't believe the ship is sinking?

When I get there, our room is empty. He isn't in the cabin, nor are his coat or life vest. Good. Uncle James must already be out on deck.

I run through the now-quiet hallway. Cabin doors stand wide open. Inside the rooms are rumpled beds, overturned suitcases, and strewn-about possessions. An elderly woman is closing a door as I pass. "Ma'am, you need to leave," I plead. "The ship is sinking!"

"We know, dear," replies the woman. Behind her, I

see an elderly man sitting in a wheelchair. "Not another thought about us, child. Be on your way!"

"But you'll die here!" I cry. *Don't they understand?*

"Hurry, girl! Go! Save yourself!" the elderly woman urges as she closes the door. I hear her turn the lock.

Hot tears run down my cold checks. I race through the hallway and up toward the second-class deck. Those poor people! What will happen to them? What if it was my nana? Will water fill the room or will the ship sink with them trapped. . . .

"Sarah! Sarah!" yells a voice behind me. Patrick! I run and hug him. It is all just too much. Too incredibly sad.

"People are going to drown, Patrick!" I whisper.

"It's terrible, I know," says Patrick. And I can tell from his face that he's seen frightening things, too. "Mary and Will weren't in their cabin."

"Let's find them outside," I say. We sprint up the stairs, go through the door out onto the deck, and step into a nightmare. The deck is filled with desperate people in a fog of panic. Kids screaming, babies crying, and men arguing. Deckhands are yelling, "Stand aside! Women and children only! Stand aside, I say!" Nearly all the lifeboats are gone. I hear a gunshot and then a whistling sound. A bright streak of red flame arcs through the sky overhead.

"Signal flares!" explains Patrick. I flinch as another flare gun goes off. Two dogs run by, terrified and barking. One slides in some water as a wave crashes over the railing. The *Titanic's* bow is tilting further down. One side is almost at the level of the sea! And somehow through it all, I hear musicians playing instruments.

Someone behind me grabs my arm. "It's now or never, young lady," growls a deckhand. He pulls me toward a lowering lifeboat.

"Wait! No!" I yell, looking over at Patrick.

"He's right, Sarah. Get in! Quickly!" urges Patrick. And I realize that he won't be let on the lifeboat. Patrick is neither a child, nor a passenger. I open my mouth, but words don't come out.

"I'm afraid. . . ." I start to say, climbing into the lifeboat. It wobbles and bumps against the side of the tilting ship. It's made of wood, but grabbing it feels like holding onto frozen metal. The sea is a very long way down.

"Here, take this," he says. Patrick reaches under his collar and then hands me his St. Christopher medal.

"I'm afraid for YOU!" I yell. The ropes start to lower the lifeboat. I put the medal around my neck, tucking it under all my layers of clothes. "Find a life vest! Find something that floats! I don't want you to drown!"

"Not a chance!" answers Patrick, trying to smile. "You saw how good a swimmer I am." The deckhand yells for people to stand back. I watch as Patrick moves away from the railing. And then he's gone.

The pulleys creak and ropes jerk as the lifeboat sinks through the air. I hold onto the bench with both hands, remembering Dorothy Gibson's gasps and white knuckles. About halfway to the water, I watch as the front rope goes slack. Then the bench slips out from under me. I'm falling through the air! I hear myself screaming and then a *splash!* as the lifeboat smacks onto the water.

An instant later, my feet hit the bench and the lifeboat lurches to one side. I plunge into the dark sea, and my scream turns to bubbles of wasted breath. The water is like knives pressed against my skin. I don't feel cold, only pain. I imagine boiling water feels the same as this frozen ocean. A picture of Patrick circling his arms in the warm pool comes to me. I kick my legs and force my arms around and around. My face breaks the surface. Taking gulps of air are like breathing in shards of glass. I open my eyes and see nothing but darkness.

REALITY CHECK

DID THE BAND REALLY PLAY ON?

Yes. Sometime after midnight, the ship's musicians began playing on deck, continuing to do so until the ship sank. Neither the bandleader, nor the seven musicians survived.

CHAPTER THIRTEEN

PATRICK

Monday, April 15; 2:00 am
in the North Atlantic Ocean

Sarah has reason to be afraid for me. I wipe a tear away. Three men are tossed overboard as a huge wave crashes over the bow. The front of the *Titanic* is dipping so far forward that people cling to railings to keep from sliding into the gurgling sea below. Voices scream for help, recite prayers, and sob out names of the lost. I need to think! Standing here being afraid is not going to help me escape. I can't find Mary and Will. I pray they found safety on a lifeboat. The ship is going to go down, and when it does, it's going to pull under whatever else is near it. That is not going to include me.

"Patrick!" yells another bellboy. He tosses me a life vest. I already have one on, but I catch it. Then I see what he is doing and copy him. I turn it upside down and step my legs into the vest's arm holes, like a big diaper. Then I tie it to my other life vest. Others are tossing deck chairs into the water. They float! I toss one in near me, but nearly slide overboard doing so. A groaning sound, like a monster twisting metal, surges up from somewhere below. I hear glass or dishes breaking. The *Titanic* is about to go under. It's time to get off.

I climb over the railing and hang onto it behind me. I look for a chair floating out in the water. That's my target. I have to get as far away from the ship as fast as possible. That's my goal. I bend my knees, take a deep breath, let go of the railing, and push off with my feet like I am diving off a cliff. Quicker than I expect, I smash into the water. The cold of it strikes my chest like a punch, forcing out all my breath. I can feel myself blacking out from the pain. I've never felt anything like this. I kick and pump my arms, swimming for the surface. My lungs ache for air. It is so dark underwater. Only my life vests seem to know which way is up. Out of breath, I can't kick any longer. The life vests drag me toward the surface. And I use my remaining strength to stop myself from inhaling salty water. *Almost there*, I tell myself. Just another second.

All of a sudden, I am gulping air and spitting seawater. I can only see a few feet in front of me. The darkness is smothering. After I catch my breath, I notice something in the water. A deck chair? No, a café table. I grab on, but my hands are so cold, they can barely grip it. I need to get up on top of the table. If I can lay across it, I won't have to hold on. It takes a thousand tries. Or at least it feels like a thousand. I stop counting after thirty or so, but I finally get myself up onto the table. Most of me, anyway. I lay on my stomach with my lower legs and feet dangling in the water. They no longer hurt. I can't feel them at all.

REALITY CHECK

Does cold water kill?

Yes. Most of those who went into the ocean didn't drown, they froze to death. It would only take 15 minutes or so to begin losing consciousness in water as cold as it was where the *Titanic* went down. Death would occur around 30 minutes.

CHAPTER FOURTEEN

SARAH

Monday, April 15; 2:15 am
in the North Atlantic Ocean

It is so dark! The sky and the sea blend together. I can't see anything except a few chunks of ice. All I hear through my water-filled ears is my thumping heart—and splashing. Realizing the life vest is holding my head above water, I stop kicking and thrashing my arms. I float! With the splashing quieted, I can hear now. Voices! "She fell in over there!" I hear a woman say. Someone on a nearby lifeboat sees me! Or at least knows I fell out of my lifeboat. I slowly raise up an arm and wave it. It feels like lifting a 50-pound sack.

"Help!" I cry with a croak. "I'm here!" My throat feels like someone has scraped it raw. Every word is painful. I hear the voices again, closer this time. And the sounds of rowing oars slice through water. I think my arm is waving, but when I look, it is still in the water. Have I even yelled? Or is that just a thought, too? I feel sleepy and confused. "Hurry," I call. But it is barely a mumble.

The next thing I remember is seeing my feet leave the water. Someone is pulling me into a lifeboat! Two women sit me between them on the middle bench. They wrap themselves around me for warmth. After a few minutes of feeling dizzy, I start to become aware again. People in the lifeboat are crying. I look out at the sea in every direction. "Where's the ship?" I ask.

"She's gone, lass," says a uniformed man rowing. "The *Titanic* just slipped under." One of the women next to me lets out a sob. *Gone?* But there are so many people still onboard! Hundreds and hundreds!

"It cracked in half!" says another woman. "I heard it breaking!" What? How? None of it makes sense. I hear their words, but can't understand. And then wreckage begins popping up on the surface of the water. Doors, deck chairs, crates, and . . . bodies.

People! Alive in the sea! Pleas for help drift across the water through the darkness. "Row that way!" I cry pointing toward the voices. Glancing around the lifeboat, I figure we can hold at least ten more people easy. "Hurry," I say, standing up. "The cold water puts you to sleep. You can't yell or wave for very long. We need to find them quickly."

"But they'll mob the boat, overturn it, and we'll all drown," says a tall woman wearing a fur coat. "It's too dangerous."

"My husband and son could be out there," says another woman. "Please, sir, row toward the cries for help." Others in the lifeboat seem to agree. Everyone knows someone left behind on the sinking ship, after all. Patrick! Could he be out there in the water, too?

"We can safely fit a few more souls," agrees a crewman. He rows toward the voices, the sound of ice chunks hitting the hull. Finding people in the dark is difficult. We pull in two young men, brothers, who tied their life vests together. Next, we find a woman with a ripped jacket in her hand. It belongs to her husband, she tells us. She was holding onto him when the ship went down. "Have you seen him in the water?" she asks. We shake our heads. There are so many beyond help.

In the distance, I see someone floating on a table. Could it be Patrick? As we row closer, it looks like a young man. But he isn't moving. When we get near to him, I can see it isn't Patrick. He isn't wearing a uniform. The shortish man grunts and lifts a hand. "He's alive!" I cry.

"He looks like a foreigner," says the tall, fur-coated woman. "Chinese or something."

The boat stops moving toward the survivor. "No reason to waste space on the likes of him," says another crewman. He starts to turn the lifeboat away from the floating man.

"Wait! But he's alive!" I yell. What does it matter what he looks like? Or where he was born? "We should help him! Please!" I beg the crewman. "Please, sir!" The crewman reluctantly nods, digging the oars into the icy water. We pull the man off the table and into the boat.

Then everyone crowds around him so he'll warm up. After a while, he can move and talk.

"Thank you," he says. Then, miraculously, he stands up and takes over rowing from the tired crewman. The cries for help grow fainter and fewer. Then there are none. The sea is silent and so are we. Everyone huddles closely together in the lifeboat, going nowhere and doing nothing. I sit on my feet, trying to feel them again. Ice crusts my wet hair. I feel both terrified and terribly sleepy. I shut my eyes and think of Patrick, Will and Mary, Uncle James, Frank, Bess, and everyone else I've met on the *Titanic*. Will any of us survive?

REALITY CHECK

DID THE LIFEBOATS PICK UP MANY SURVIVORS?

No. Most lifeboats rowed away from the *Titanic* as it was sinking and didn't go back.

WAS A CHINESE MAN REALLY RESCUED FROM THE WATER?

Yes, only two out of twenty lifeboats turned back to rescue survivors from the water. Lifeboat #14 (reluctantly) picked up Fang Lang of Hong Kong, who did help row once he regained his strength.

CHAPTER FIFTEEN

PATRICK

Monday, April 15; 2:15 am
in the North Atlantic Ocean

The table rocks and bobs under me. My eyes adjust to the darkness and sounds reach my ears, too. Horrible screams and cries, crashing and shattering noises, and the slow creaking groan of twisting metal. I paddle with my hands to turn myself toward the uproar. And there she is, the *Titanic*, in a fight for her life with the sea. Her lights flicker off, then on, and then off for good.

The front end of the dark ship dips down now and is soon completely underwater. The stern sticks up in the air! Its propeller dangles high above the water's surface. People, equipment, and anything not tied down is sliding off into the sea. The insides of the ship are tumbling forward, too. I can hear breaking glass, snapping wood, and bending metal. And then the weight of so much seawater is too much for the giant ship. She breaks in half. Snapped in two like a twig in mud. The bow slips under the water as the stern slams back down onto the surface. Then it fills with the sea and tips back up, its propeller once more turning in the air. And then it's gone, too. The *Titanic* has sunk.

After an eerie silence, I can hear cries for help. Surely people are being rescued! Sarah said that lifeboats had launched half full. "Help!" I yell. It is so hard to see in the dark. "Help me!"

"Swim this way! Over here," says a voice across the water. I paddle with my hands and try to kick my numb legs. I can see it now. It's one of the collapsible lifeboats, a small boat made of canvas, not wood. It is upside down, but floating. People are pulling themselves up onto it. I kick and paddle. *You can make it,* I tell myself. Just a little farther! Finally, I hear the front of the table bump the hull. I drag my chest and hips from the tabletop onto the overturned boat. A crouched man grabs under my armpits and tugs, falling backward. "Easy there, Patrick," he says. "I got you."

"Frank!" It's the guard. He sits me down beside him and wraps a big arm around my shoulders. "You saved me, Frank." Tears sting my eyes.

"None of us is saved yet, lad," Frank says. He's right. I count ten survivors squatting on the hull. Everyone is soaking wet. One young man looks hurt. He holds an arm like it's injured.

"What do we do now?" I ask Frank. I pull my knees up to my chest and tuck my head down. Ice is already forming on my life vest. I can't feel my hands or feet at all.

"We wait," he says. And no one speaks another word. Talking takes energy. Opening my mouth lets in cold. So we just sit. In the dark. In silence. In the middle of the North Atlantic Ocean.

Hours pass. But the darkness continues. At some point, I lift my head in time to see the faint light of a distant signal flare. A rescue ship is out there! But how far away is it? And how long will it take for it to find us? "Hurry," I pray.

The longest night of my life is finally ending. The sky is getting light on the horizon. As the sun rises, it turns the floating chunks of ice pink and gold. And then I see the most beautiful sight of my life. A ship! I can see it clearly. It has stopped alongside a lifeboat. People are climbing up ladders made of rope. On its side is a name: *Carpathia*. "We're rescued!" I say.

Heads around me lift, eyes squint in the growing daylight. I try to stand up, but my legs are numb. The young man with the hurt arm gets to his feet. He starts yelling and waving. "Over here!" he hollers. Someone else struggles up and joins in. I want to stand up, too! I keep leaning over, trying to get my legs under me. But it isn't working. And with all the commotion, our overturned lifeboat is rocking. When I lean again, I lose my balance and tumble down the side of the hull. With a splash, I sink into the sea, the light of the surface fading away quickly.

REALITY CHECK

Did the Titanic really break in half?

Yes. The fact was debated for years until ocean explorer Robert Ballard found the *Titanic* on the seafloor in 1985 in two pieces.

CHAPTER SIXTEEN

SARAH

Monday, April 15, 1912; 7:00 am
onboard the *Carpathia*

We are rescued! A crewman grabs me at the top of a rope ladder and lifts me into the ship. A female passenger takes me to her cabin. I change out of my wet, icy clothes and into a nightshirt she gives me. Then I get into bed and she packs hot water bottles all around me. Warmth! I thought I'd never feel it again. The woman brings me some soup and milky tea. And then I sleep the rest of the day and through the night.

I wake up Tuesday morning alone and in a panic. Where am I? What's happened? And it all comes flooding back. The *Titanic* has sunk! All those people in the water! Where are Patrick and his cousins? What about Uncle James? My clothes lay over a chair, completely dried. I change and leave the cabin. I follow the sounds of voices to a large, open room filled with people. It smells of musty blankets and hot tea.

"You're awake, child!" exclaims someone behind me. It is the kind woman whose cabin I slept in. I thank her.

"I need to find my uncle and my friends," I say. Looking around, I don't recognize anyone in the room. "Is this the only ship with the *Titanic's* survivors?" She looks at me with sad eyes.

"There was great loss of life," she says quietly. "All survivors are onboard the *Carpathia*." I follow her to the ship's office. There, a man asks for my name, class of travel, home address, port of departure, and my travel companions.

"James Colvin, sir, my uncle," I say. The officer checks some lists. He doesn't find the name. Has Uncle James not survived? The officer starts writing a message on a slip of paper.

"What about Patrick Kelley? And Mary and Will?"

I gulp. I realize I don't know anyone's last name but Patrick's. "Kelley with two *es*."

"I'm sorry, miss. No record of Patrick Kelley. But ask around on the ship. Not everyone is accounted for," he says. Then he hands me what he's written. "Take this to the wireless room. The telegraph operator will message your parents."

I slowly walk in the direction the officer has pointed to. But I can barely think. Everything feels unreal. I give the message to the telegraph operator and wander the ship. A few men wear White Star uniforms. I ask each one about Patrick. Many know who he is, but no one has seen him. "There's not a bellboy among the survivors, miss," says one.

Alone. Never have I felt so alone. I look everywhere for a familiar face among the new widows, penniless immigrants, and orphaned children.

"Mary!" I cry. It's Mary! She's alive! We hug for a long time. When I ask about Will, she only bites her lip and shakes her head. They'd both made it out of third class and up onto the deck, Mary tells me. But the deckhands only let Mary in a lifeboat.

"I left my brother standing on the deck. The sea was covering his shoes," Mary says with a sob. "I've not seen cousin Patrick either." We hug again, and I notice a nasty-looking cut on Mary's forehead. "I slipped getting out of the lifeboat," she explains. "It's nothing."

"A crewman told me there's a doctor on board," I mention. "Maybe he has a bandage." We make our way through the small ship to the doctor's cabin. The door is open. Inside are beds so close together, they're nearly on top of one another. One person has a leg up, like it's broken. A pregnant woman sits in another bed. A few others are in chairs with hands and feet wrapped in bandages. Off in a corner, someone is asleep with hot water bottles all around him. His red hair catches the sunlight coming through the window. It's Patrick! He's alive!

REALITY CHECK

HOW MANY PEOPLE SURVIVED THE SINKING OF THE TITANIC?

Of the more than 2,200 passengers and crew onboard the *Titanic*, only 705 survived. All were picked up by the *Carpathia*.

DID ANY BELLBOYS REALLY SURVIVE?

No. Less than one quarter of all 908 crew members lived. Over sixty percent of first-class passengers survived.

CHAPTER SEVENTEEN

PATRICK

Thursday, April 18, 1912; onboard the *Carpathia*

"It's pretty severe frostbite," says the doctor looking at my purplish toes. Parts of my feet are still numb after two days in bed. And other parts hurt when I try to walk. That's a good sign, according to the doctor. It means they are healing. Everyone on *Carpathia* is so generous. They feed us and dry our clothes in their ovens. A crewman even made me a set of crutches! Mary and Sarah keep me company. They made sure my parents received word that I survived. Father will be too relieved to be angry. I can already hear Mother saying, "I told you it was dangerous!" She was right. So many people lost. It's hard to believe. How can a ship the size of a town disappear just like that? I shudder at the memory of it.

"Hurry up, Patrick!" teases Sarah. She helps me move onto the deck and lean against a railing. "There it is!" Guiding us to shore is the Statue of Liberty. We've reached New York City. Lots of passengers have come up onto the deck to see Lady Liberty, as Sarah calls her. She is a welcoming sight. Hello, America!

"We're going to start filming right away," says a voice behind us. I see Sarah's eyes double in size. It is the film star Dorothy Gibson talking to the *Carpathia's* captain. "The title will be *Saved From the* Titanic." Sarah's mouth drops open in disbelief, then closes tight. Miss Gibson and the captain stroll on.

"What a terrible idea," scolds Sarah.

"The pictures in my mind are bad enough, too," I agree. Dorothy Gibson just lost a fan, I think. Then I reach into my pocket. "Here's my address in Ireland. I'm going to need a new copy of yours." Sarah pulls a folded piece of paper from her coat and hands it to me. "What's in it?" I ask. It is thick and rattles when I shake it.

"Open it," she says. And I do. It is my St. Christopher medal. "Make sure to wear it on the ship going home." Not that I will be going back to Ireland right away. Mary promises to nurse me back to health first in New York City. I am in no rush to head across the cold North Atlantic Ocean again. I put the medal around my neck, tucking it under my collar.

"You're a believer in Irish superstitions, now?" I tease. Sarah looks out at the sea. I can imagine what she sees.

"We are lucky to be alive, aren't we?" Sarah says.

"That we are," I say. "Lucky indeed."

REALITY CHECK

Was there really a movie made right after the Titanic *sank?* Yes! *Saved from the* Titanic, starring Dorothy Gibson, was released May 14, 1912.

Saved From The Titanic

ECLAIR'S EXCLUSIVE EXTRA

A Startling Story of the Sea's Greatest Tragedy By Miss **DOROTHY GIBSON**, A Survivor

SHE IS SUPPORTED BY A POWERFUL CAST

Six Color and Gold Posters, Herald's Photos

A FILM WITHOUT A PARALLEL

TUESDAY MAY 14 — **Eclair Film Co.** FORT LEE, N. J. SALES COMPANY, Sole Agents — TUESDAY MAY 14

CHAPTER EIGHTEEN

SARAH

June 21, 1912;
Boston, Massachusetts

Help! Over here! This way! Help! I row a lifeboat in icy water. No one is there, but the pleas go on. *Help! Save us!*

I awake from a familiar dream, shivering in a cold sweat. Warm sunlight streams in my window. I gulp down a half-full glass of water next to my bed. "It was just a dream," I remind myself. "I'm safe. I'm home."

Tiny mewing sounds come from under my bed. I kneel down and pet the mama cat and each of her four kittens. The stray cat started hanging around the day I left Ireland, Mother claims. Begging for scraps to feed her growing belly and making friends with our pup, Puck! After I got home, she snuck in the house and had her kittens under my bed. I named her Jenny.

Two months have passed since Father met me at the dock in New York. I've never been hugged so tight for so long. He didn't let me out of his sight the entire train ride back to Boston. And he kept telling me how sorry he was. Sorry? Sorry for what? I survived. I told him all about Patrick, Mary, and poor lost Will. I sang Father a couple of the Irish songs I learned, too. His eyes sparkled with remembrance and he joined in on one or two. He isn't a great singer.

For weeks after I returned, the newspapers were filled with *Titanic* news and stories. Kids in the neighborhood keep asking me about it. It got worse when everyone saw Dorothy Gibson in *Saved from the Titanic*. Everyone wants to know if the film was true to life. I told everyone I hadn't seen it, so I couldn't say. Which is true enough.

"Sarah! Breakfast is ready!" Mother calls. I dress and go to the table. Next to my plate is an envelope. The stamp is Irish! The return address says Mr. Patrick

J. Kelley. I rip it open, unfold the paper inside, and something shiny falls out. It is a St. Christopher medal.

Dear Sarah,

I arrived safely in Ireland. It is good to be home! My feet have healed. A couple of toes hurt when it's cold, but not too bad. Please accept this small gift. I wouldn't want my Irish-American little sister to travel without one. Please write back soon!

Yours truly,

Patrick

I put the St. Christopher medal on, tucking it under my blouse. I pick up my toast and begin to eat. I'm thankful for my luck—thankful to have escaped the *Titanic*.

REALITY CHECK

Was the Titanic *really in the news a lot?*

Yes! There were official investigations by both the British and American governments. Laws were changed to require ocean liners to have enough lifeboats for all passengers. Ship designs were improved to make hulls stronger. And the International Ice Patrol was created to track icebergs in the North Atlantic.

TIMELINE

July 1908—Design of the *Titanic* is approved.

Spring 1909—Construction of the *Titanic* begins in Belfast, Ireland.

1910—The decision is made to only install 20 lifeboats on the *Titanic*: 16 standard boats and 4 collapsible ones.

April 9, 1912—Officer David Blair is replaced at the last minute and leaves the *Titanic*, mistakenly taking with him the key to the locker where the binoculars are kept.

April 10, 1912—The *Titanic* sets sail from Southampton, England.

April 11, 1912—The *Titanic* picks up passengers in Cherbourg, France, and Queenstown, Ireland.

April 14, 1912
- Seven different iceberg warnings are received throughout the day.
- 11:40 p.m.: Lookout crew spots an iceberg dead ahead. The *Titanic* swerves and the iceberg scrapes across the right side of the ship's bow, shaving off rivet heads and opening up the hull. In just ten minutes, the front part of the ship takes on a massive amount of water.

April 15, 1912
- 12:05 a.m.: The order is given to prepare the lifeboats.
- 12:25 a.m.: Women and children (as well as some men) start boarding the lifeboats. Meanwhile, nearly 60 miles away, the *Carpathia* receives the *Titanic's* distress call.
- 2:05 a.m.: The last lifeboat departs, leaving more than 1,500 passengers still aboard the sinking ship.
- 2:17 a.m.: Captain Smith tells the crew, "It's every man for himself." The evacuation of passengers is over.
- 2:20 a.m.: The *Titanic* breaks in half and the bow sinks. The stern fills with water and also sinks a few minutes later.
- 4:10 a.m.: The *Carpathia* arrives and begins rescuing passengers from lifeboats.
- 8:50 a.m.: 705 survivors are now aboard the *Carpathia*.

April 18, 1912—The *Carpathia* arrives in New York Harbor.

FIND OUT MORE

Adams, Simon. *Titanic*. England: London: DK Children, 2004.
From its famous passengers to the exploration of its remains, learn the full story of this tragic ship in this eyewitness book.

Hopkinson, Deborah. *Titanic: Voices From the Disaster*. New York City: Scholastic Inc., 2012.
Hear the true stories of the real survivors and witnesses in this award-winning book.

Korman, Gordon. *Unsinkable, Collision Course,* and *S.O.S.* New York City: Scholastic Inc., 2011.
Join the three-book adventure!

Ohlin, Nancy. *The Titanic (Blast Back!)*. New York City: Little Bee Books, 2016.
What was life really like on the *Titanic*?

Pierce, Nicola. *Spirit of the Titanic*. Ireland: Dublin: The O'Brien Press, 2013.
A terrific tale of the ghost of a teen who died while building the *Titanic*. He haunts the ship to warn its Irish immigrant passengers.

Zullo, Alan. *Titanic: Young Survivors*. New York City: Scholastic Inc., 2015.
Find about how ten real young people managed to survive.

SELECTED BIBLIOGRAPHY

Ballard, Robert D. *The Discovery of the Titanic*. Toronto: Warner/Madison Press, 1988.

Brown, David G. *The Last Log of the Titanic*. New York City: International Marine/Ragged Mountain Press, 2000.

Davie, Michael. *Titanic: The Death and Life of a Legend*. New York City: Vintage, 2012.

Lord, Walter. *A Night to Remember*. New York City: Griffin, 2005.

McCarty, Jennifer H. *What Really Sank the Titanic: New Forensic Discoveries*. New York City: Citadel, 2008.

Wels, Susan. *Titanic: Legacy of the World's Greatest Ocean Liner*. Alexandria: Time-Life Education, 1997.